The
United States

by Robin S. Doak

Content Adviser: Alex Lubin,
Assistant Professor of American Studies,
University of New Mexico

Reading Adviser: Dr. Linda D. Labbo,
Department of Reading Education,
College of Education, The University of Georgia

COMPASS POINT BOOKS
MINNEAPOLIS, MINNESOTA

FIRST REPORTS

Compass Point Books
3109 West 50th Street, #115
Minneapolis, MN 55410

Visit Compass Point Books on the Internet at *www.compasspointbooks.com*
or e-mail your request to *custserv@compasspointbooks.com*

On the cover: Grand Teton National Park in Jackson Hole, Wyoming

Photographs ©:John Elk III, cover; Creatas, 4; Digital Vision, 5; PhotoDisc, 7, 8, 20, 23, 29, 31, 33, 34, 36; Hulton/Archive by Getty Images, 9, 10, 12, 13, 14, 15, 16, 17, 27, 35, 37; Courtesy of the Director, National Army Museum, London, 11; Flip Schulke/Corbis, 18; David McNew/Getty Images, 19; Comstock, 21; Corbis, 22, 40; Raymond Gehman/Corbis, 24; James P. Rowan, 25, 30, 39; David Falconer, 26; Joe Raedle/Newsmakers/Getty Images, 28; Bill Pugliano/Getty Images, 32; Bob Krist/Corbis, 38; Jim Baron/The Image Finders, 41; Michael Smith/Getty Images, 42–43.

Editor: Patricia Stockland
Photo Researcher: Marcie C. Spence
Designer/Page Production: Bradfordesign, Inc./Biner Design
Cartographer: XNR Productions, Inc.

Library of Congress Cataloging-in-Publication Data
Doak, Robin S. (Robin Santos), 1963–
    United States of America / by Robin S. Doak.
        p. cm. — (First reports)
    Summary: Introduces the geography, history, culture, and people of the United States of America.
    Includes bibliographical references and index.
    ISBN 0-7565-0583-6
    1. United States—Juvenile literature. [1. United States.] I. Title. II. Series.
    E156.D6 2004
    973—dc22   2003014433

Table of Contents

NOTE: In this book, words that are defined in the glossary are
in **bold** the first time they appear in the text.

Welcome to the United States

▲ *Americans have many different beliefs and backgrounds.*

Hello! Hola! Konichi wa! You might hear any one of these English, Spanish, and Japanese greetings in the United States. Nearly all Americans speak English. Many other languages are spoken in the United States, too.

Not all Americans are the same. People in the United States belong to many different ethnic groups.

They practice different religions and have different beliefs, yet they strive to overcome their differences.

The United States is on the continent of North America. It is the third largest country in the world. Only Russia and Canada are larger in size. The United States is bordered by Canada to the north and Mexico to the south. It stretches nearly 3,000 miles (4,800 kilometers) between the Pacific Ocean to the west and the Atlantic Ocean to the east.

▲ *The United States is a large country with farms and cities, mountains and plains.*

The United States is divided into 50 states. Forty-eight of the states are connected to one another. These states are sometimes called the contiguous or lower 48 states. Two states, Alaska and Hawaii, are not connected to the mainland. The capital of the

▲ *Map of the United States, including state capitals*

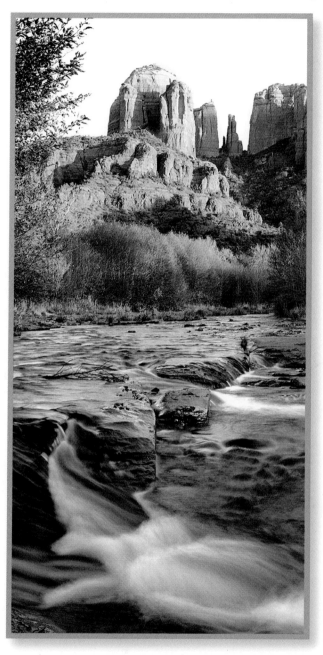

▲ *The varied landscape of Sedona, Arizona*

United States is Washington, D.C. It is not a part of any state.

The land of the United States is as varied as its people. It ranges from tall, rugged mountain ranges to vast, hot deserts—with everything in between. There are big cities and small towns. Some areas are good for farming, while other areas are centers of **industry.**

▲ *Buffalo are native to the United States and once roamed freely on the plains.*

The United States is also home to many different types of animals and plants. Animals include bald eagles, buffalo, bears, deer, moose, and alligator. On the West Coast, one might see giant redwood and sequoia forests. On the East Coast, pine, birch, maple, and oak trees are common. To help protect these plants and animals, huge areas of land have been set aside as national parks.

Colonial America

Native Americans were the first people to live in the area now known as the United States. By the early 1600s, millions of native people lived in all parts of North America. There were many different tribes. Each tribe had its own language and customs.

▲ *A shaman, or Native American doctor, around 1550, before the arrival of many Europeans*

▲ *Jamestown was the first permanent settlement founded by the British.*

In 1607, people from England founded the first permanent European settlement in the United States. The settlement in Virginia was named Jamestown. Thirteen years later, a ship called the *Mayflower* reached the coast of what is now Massachusetts. On board were a group of people called the Pilgrims. The Pilgrims founded Plymouth Colony, a place where they could freely practice their Puritan religion.

During the next few decades, more and more people from England came to live in North America. Thirteen colonies existed along the Atlantic Coast by 1733. These colonies were under the power of Great Britain and its king.

By the early 1770s, many Americans had become unhappy with British rule. These Americans wanted to have more control over their businesses and their political system. In 1775, the Revolutionary War between Great Britain and the 13 colonies began.

▲ *The first battle of the Revolutionary War happened in Massachusetts on Lexington Common.*

A year later, the colonies signed the Declaration of Independence. The document declared that the colonies were now free from Great Britain.

The Revolutionary War officially ended in 1783 with victory for the colonies. Six years later, the Constitution was written. The Constitution is a **document** that outlines how the U.S. government is organized. The Constitution has served to guide the nation for more than 200 years. Some changes have been made over the years. These changes are called amendments.

▲ *The signing of the Constitution played an important part in building the United States.*

Growth and War

▲ *The Rocky Mountains loom in the distance as pioneers move west.*

The early 1800s were a time of great growth for the United States. As the Northeast became more crowded, people began moving west. The new lands offered space and resources to support the growing population. Native Americans lived throughout these areas. The pioneers often relied on them for food and guidance.

In 1803, President Thomas Jefferson purchased the Louisiana Territory for the United States. This more than doubled the land area of the country. By 1865, the United States had grown from 13 states to 36.

As the nation grew, one issue threatened to divide it: slavery. During the 1600s and 1700s, American slave traders had kidnapped people from Africa. The Africans were brought to the United States to work on farms in the South. The Africans were not given any rights and did not earn wages for their hard work.

By the early 1800s, many people in the North wanted to do away with slavery. People in the South disagreed. In early 1861, most Southern states had seceded, or split apart, from

▲ *Africans working as slaves in a Southern cotton field around 1850*

▲ *The North and the South fought each other over slavery, an issue that almost destroyed the nation.*

the United States. They formed a new nation called the Confederate States of America.

The war between the North and the South is called the Civil War. From 1861 to 1865, thousands of Americans died fighting one another. The war ended when the South surrendered.

Moving into the Future

During the 20th century, the United States continued to grow and become stronger.

The 1900s were also a time of great distress for the nation. During that time, the United States suffered through a serious economic crisis. The Great Depression of the 1930s caused millions of Americans to lose their jobs, homes, and savings. The Depression lasted for more than a decade.

▲ *During the Great Depression of the 1930s, many families packed up their belongings and headed west in search of work.*

▲ *Production of supplies for World War II, such as these planes at a Lockheed plant in 1943, helped end the Great Depression.*

During the 1900s, the United States fought in two World Wars. Thousands of Americans lost their lives while fighting for world peace. The American involvement in World War II (1939–1945) helped bring an end to the Depression and the war.

▲ The fight for equality by civil rights activists made the United States a better place for everyone.

Within the nation, the descendants of slaves struggled to win equality and the freedom to vote. Their struggle was called the civil rights movement.

Today, the United States is stronger than ever. It is a top industrial country, producing goods that are sold here and around the world. Most Americans enjoy a good standard of living, although there is still poverty in the nation. Some groups are still treated unfairly on the basis of their race, gender, or religion.

▲ *The United States produces goods that are used around the world.*

The Northeast

The Northeast is made up of 11 states. Maine, New Hampshire, Vermont, Massachusetts, Connecticut, and Rhode Island are part of an area called New England. New York, New Jersey, Pennsylvania, Maryland, and Delaware are known as the Middle Atlantic states.

The Northeast is a center of business, art, and education. In the early 1800s, the U.S. Industrial Revolution began here. This was the change from goods being made by hand in small amounts to goods being made with new technology in large quantities. Since that time,

▲ *A fountain near Philadelphia City Hall*

factories in the Northeast have made goods that have helped the nation grow. Because the region is along the Atlantic Ocean, shipping these goods has been easy. The Northeast is also home to the nation's first universities and museums.

The two largest cities in the Northeast are New York City, New York, and Philadelphia, Pennsylvania. New York City, nicknamed the Big Apple, is also the largest city in the United States. Philadelphia was the nation's first capital. Both cities are important transportation centers.

◀ *Ticker tape parades in New York City are held to celebrate big events.*

The Southeast

The Southeast is made up of 12 states. These states are Alabama, Arkansas, Florida, Georgia, Kentucky, Louisiana, Mississippi, North Carolina, South Carolina, Tennessee, Virginia, and West Virginia.

The Southeast's rich, fertile land and mild climate make it a perfect place for growing crops. Crops grown here include cotton, sugar, tobacco, and peanuts.

Tourism is an important part of the Southeast's

▲ *The Southeast is a good place to grow crops.*

economy. Warm winters and many miles of coastline draw people from around the world. One state that relies on tourism is Florida. The state is home to many attractions that draw millions of visitors each year.

▲ *Miami Beach is a popular tourist destination in Florida.*

The largest cities in the Southeast are Jacksonville, Florida, and Memphis, Tennessee. Jacksonville is an important port for automobile transports. Memphis is located on the Mississippi River. For centuries, it has been an important trade stop.

▲ *The DeSoto Bridge crosses the Mississippi River in Memphis, Tennessee. The city is an important location for trade.*

The Southwest

▲ *Saguaro National Park near Tuscon, Arizona, shows a variety of plants and landscape.*

The Southwest is made up of four states. These states are Arizona, New Mexico, Oklahoma, and Texas. With a climate that is warm and dry year-round, the region attracts more people every year. It is one of the fastest-growing areas in the United States.

The Southwest is home to many different types of land. In New Mexico and Arizona, for example, you can find hot, dry deserts. In Oklahoma, you may see miles of fertile plains and green fields. Beautiful sandy beaches along the coast of Texas attract swimmers and nature lovers.

The Southwest has a long, rich history. For nearly three centuries, the region was controlled by the Spanish. Later, it was the territory of Mexico. In 1848, the United States took control of the Southwest. Later, the U.S. government forced thousands of

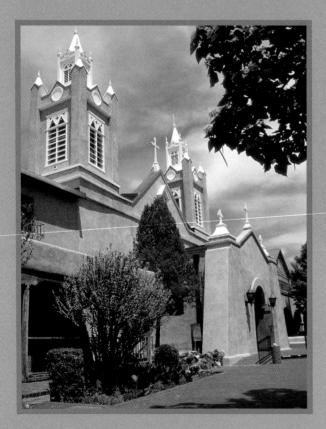

△ *Spanish architecture such as the San Felipe de Neri church in Albuquerque, New Mexico, can still be seen in the Southwest.*

▲ *Navajo women weaving with a loom near Monument Valley, Arizona*

Native Americans onto reservations in the area. Today, many native people live in the Southwest. Some of these Native Americans live on **reservations** or pueblos, while others live in larger cities.

The Southwest is important to the nation's economic health. Oil and natural gas are found here. Farmland and ranches in the region are a top source of food for people throughout the United States.

Several big cities are located in the Southwest. Two of the largest are Houston, Texas, and Phoenix, Arizona. Located near the Gulf of Mexico, Houston is home to one of the busiest ports in the United States. Phoenix is one of the fastest-growing cities in the country.

▲ *Oil and natural gas are found in the Southwest.*

The Midwest

▲ *Dairy cattle rest on a farm in Wisconsin.*

The Midwest is made up of 12 states. These states are Illinois, Indiana, Iowa, Kansas, Michigan, Minnesota, Missouri, Nebraska, North Dakota, Ohio, South Dakota, and Wisconsin.

The Midwest is called the breadbasket of the nation. It produces most of the nation's grain. That is because of the region's fertile soil. Wheat, corn, soybeans, and other crops are grown here. The Midwest is rich in other natural resources. Iron, lead, coal, and granite can all be found here, too. The Midwest is also known for its many industries. The area produces steel, rubber, automobiles, ships, and aircraft.

Many big rivers flow through the Midwest. One of the most important is the Mississippi River. This

▲ *The Mississippi River cuts through the Midwest.*
It is a useful means of transporting goods.

mighty waterway measures 2,350 miles (3,760 km). It stretches from northwest Minnesota all the way to the Gulf of Mexico. The Midwest is also home to some of the Great Lakes.

▲ *The skyscrapers of downtown Chicago offer a great view of the city and Lake Michigan.*

The two largest cities in the Midwest are Chicago, Illinois, and Detroit, Michigan. Both cities are major centers of business and trade. Chicago is located on Lake Michigan, one of the Great Lakes. Detroit, located on the Detroit River, is known for automobile production.

▲ Dearborn, Michigan, is home to a Ford assembly plant. Automobile production has been an important part of business in the Midwest.

The West

The West is made up of 11 states. Nine of the states are connected on the North American mainland. These states are California, Colorado, Idaho, Montana, Nevada, Oregon, Utah, Washington, and Wyoming.

Two of the 11 states are not connected to the rest of the Western states. One state, Hawaii, is a group of islands located in the central Pacific Ocean. Hawaii is

▲ *Hawaii, a group of islands, is not connected to the rest of the United States.*

more than 2,000 miles (3,200 km) away from the U.S. mainland. Canada separates the other state, Alaska, from the lower 48 states.

The land of the West is varied and unique. There are tall, rugged mountains and hot, dry deserts. There are also rain forests, beaches, **tundra,** canyons, and volcanoes. The area's natural beauty makes it very popular with tourists.

The climate in the West also varies. Hawaii, for example, has a wet, tropical climate. The average temperature there year-round

▲ *People enjoy camping in the mountains of the West.*

is 75 degrees Fahrenheit (24 degrees Celsius). Alaska has a dry, Arctic climate. In the wintertime, temperatures there can drop to as low as minus 60 F (minus 51 C). On the mainland, the West's climate ranges from **temperate** in the northernmost states to **semitropical** in southern California.

◄ *Panning for gold in California around 1855*

The West has always been known for its many natural resources. In 1848, the discovery of gold in California caused people to flock to the region. Other valuable resources there include fish, timber, and minerals.

▲ *San Diego is an important port for the United States.*

The two largest cities in the West are Los Angeles, California, and San Diego, California. Both cities are important international ports. American goods are shipped out of the ports. Items from around the world enter the United States there.

People of the United States

Many people live in the United States. Only China and India have more people.

One of the nation's greatest strengths is the **diversity** of its people. For more than 400 years, people from all parts of the world have come to live in the United States. Together, these people have

▲ *Ellis Island in New York was the gateway to the United States for many immigrants.*

helped build a strong nation. People continue to come to the United States. Each year, hundreds of thousands of people migrate here, looking for freedom and a better life.

A majority of Americans are white. The United States also has growing African-American, Latino, and Asian populations. In the United States, people are free to worship as they please. As a result, there are many different religions in the United States. More than half of all Americans are Protestant. Many of the earliest settlements were founded by Protestants.

Many Americans may be Roman Catholic, Jewish, Muslim, or other faiths, too.

◀ People in the United States are free to practice whatever religion they choose. Freedom is very important to Americans.

▲ *People relax in Chicago's Lincoln Park. Many Americans enjoy outdoor activities.*

Americans are hard workers, but they also like to enjoy themselves. Americans have plenty of ways to relax in their free time. There are movie theaters, museums, and art galleries. Most big cities have their own ballet, opera, and theater companies. For those who enjoy outdoor activities, there are many parks, beaches, and national parks in every state.

Americans observe a number of holidays. One of the most festive is Independence Day. On July 4, Americans around the nation celebrate the signing of the Declaration of Independence in 1776. Picnics, parades, and fireworks displays are all part of the fun.

▲ *Fireworks explode over the Lincoln Memorial and Washington Monument on July 4.*

▲ *Americans love baseball. It has been called the nation's pastime.*

Americans love sports. They like to play sports in their spare time. Many also like to cheer for their favorite professional sports teams. The most popular sport is baseball. The first baseball team was probably organized in New York City in 1842.

Other popular professional sports include football, basketball, and hockey. Most big cities have a professional team to call their own. Each year, the best professional teams compete for top honors in their sport. These championship games are watched on television by millions of people.

As you visit different regions of the United States, you will see that the nation has something for everyone. *Goodbye, adios,* and *sayonara* are just a few ways the friendly people of the United States will wish you well after a visit to their part of the country.

◀ *Rodeos are popular events that celebrate cowboy traditions and Americans' love of freedom.*

Glossary

diversity—a group of people with different races and cultures

document—a paper that contains important information

industry—a business that makes products

reservations—large areas of land set aside for Native Americans; in Canada, reservations are called reserves

semitropical—an environment in or near a tropical zone

temperate—a rain forest environment that has a cooler climate

tundra—treeless land in the north where the ground stays frozen most of the year

Did You Know?

- The largest state in the United States is Alaska. It has 570,374 square miles (1,477,269 sq km) of land. It accounts for more than one-fifth of the nation's total size. The smallest state is Rhode Island. It is just 1,045 square miles (2,717 sq km).

- Washington, D.C., has been the nation's capital since 1800. Named after George Washington, the capital was built on land given to the government by the states of Virginia and Maryland.

- Puerto Rico is part of the United States, but it is not a state. It is a commonwealth. This means it rules itself, but it has ties to the United States. Another U.S. commonwealth is the Northern Mariana Islands.

At a Glance

Official Name: United States of America

Capital: Washington, D.C.

Official language: None; majority speaks English, Spanish

National anthem: "The Star-Spangled Banner"

Area: 3,717,811 square miles (9,666,309 sq km)

Highest point: Mount McKinley, 20,320 feet (6,198 meters)

Lowest point: Death Valley, 282 feet (86 meters) below sea level

Population: 295,734,134 (2005 estimate)

Head of government: President

Money: U.S. dollar

Important Dates

1607	The Jamestown settlement is founded in Virginia.
1620	Pilgrims found Plymouth Colony in Massachusetts.
1775– 1783	During the American Revolution, American colonists win their freedom from Great Britain.
1803	The Louisiana Purchase more than doubles the size of the United States.
1812– 1814	Americans fight the War of 1812 with Great Britain.
1861– 1865	The Civil War between the North and South costs thousands of Americans their lives and devastates the South. The war ends when the South surrenders.
1917	The United States enters World War I (1914–1918).
1929	The Great Depression begins in the United States.
1941	The United States enters World War II (1939–1945)
1969	U.S. astronauts land on the moon.
2001	Terrorists attack the World Trade Center in New York and the Pentagon in Washington, D.C. More than 3,000 people are killed in the attacks.

Want to Know More?

At the Library

Burger, James P. *The Library of the Westward Expansion*. New York: Powerkids Press, 2002.

Guthrie, Woody. *This Land Is Your Land*. Boston: Little, Brown & Co., 1998.

Hoose, Philip. *We Were There Too!: Young People in U.S. History*. New York: Farrar Straus & Giroux, 2001.

Raatma, Lucia. *Ellis Island*. Minneapolis: Compass Point Books, 2002.

Rappaport, Doreen. *Freedom River*. New York: Jump at the Sun, 2000.

On the Web

For more information on The United States, use FactHound to track down Web sites related to this book.

1. Go to *www.compasspointbooks.com/facthound*
2. Type in this book ID: 0756505836
3. Click on the *Fetch It* button.

Your trusty FactHound will fetch the best Web sites for you!

On the Road

Smithsonian Institution
National Mall
Washington, DC 20013
For a peek into "America's Attic," a museum of U.S. history, culture, science, and art

Through the Mail

National Cowboy & Western Heritage Museum
1700 N.E. 63rd St.
Oklahoma City, OK 73111
info@nationalcowboymuseum.org
For information on America's Wild West and its history

Index

About the Author

Robin S. Doak has been writing for children for more than 14 years. A former editor of Weekly Reader and U*S*Kids magazine, Ms. Doak has authored fun and educational materials for kids of all ages. Some of her work includes biographies of explorers such as Henry Hudson and John Smith, as well as other titles in this series. Ms. Doak is a past winner of the Educational Press Association of America Distinguished Achievement Award. She lives with her husband and three children in central Connecticut.